Daddy Hairdo

For my dAughter, CaRys ~ Fm

For DAD, my HAIR-O ~ CP

SIMON & SCHUSTER
First published in Great Britain in 2018 by Simon & Schuster UK Ltd
1st Floor, 222 Gray's Inn Road, London, WC1X 8HB
A CBS Company

Text copyright © 2018 Francis Martin
Illustrations copyright © 2018 Claire Powell

ISBN: 978-1-4711-4786-9 (HB) • ISBN: 978-1-4711-4787-6 (PB) • ISBN: 978-1-4711-4788-3 (eBook)
Printed in China • 10 9 8 7 6 5 4 3 2 1

Daddy Hairdo

FRANCIS MARTIN   CLAIRE POWELL

SIMON & SCHUSTER
London   New York   Sydney   Toronto   New Delhi

When Amy was born,
she didn't have much hair.

Dad, on the other hand,

had LOTS.

Then Amy and Dad had the same amount of hair.

Then Amy had more hair than Dad and Dad's hair just started . . .

disappearing.

Amy tried to help Dad look for it

but it had gone.

For good.

Amy and Dad looked in books.
Where does hair go when it goes?

Does it go off around the world . . .

in search of hair-raising adventures?

Or does it just disappear
down the plughole?

Dad's missing hair
was nowhere to be found.

But in the meantime,
Amy's hair grew . . .

and grew . . .

and GREW.

Just look at it all!

It took **a lot** of looking after.

On windy days,

it was a right nuisance.

When it got tangled,
the cat had to comb it.

On rainy days, it got so wet
Amy had to dry it on a washing line.

And when she played hide-and-seek,

Amy was **ALWAYS** found.

Soon, it was so long she couldn't even stand on the floor any more and had to be carried around.

In spite of all this, Amy **loved** her hair. She wasn't going to go to just any hairdresser.

DAD would have to think of something.

So he studied . . .

and he practised . . .

until finally he was
ready to reveal . . .

. . . the Daddy Hairdo!

Dad created . . .

'The Ice Cream Cone',

'The Rings of Saturn',

'The Castle in the Clouds'

and, his personal favourite,

'The Triple Beehive'.

Amy was a sensation!

And Dad's hairdos were
the talk of the town.

Everybody loved them.

But 'The Castle in the Clouds' made hide-and-seek even **MORE** difficult . . .

there were some places that
'The Ice Cream Cone' wasn't allowed into . . .

. . . and, worst of all, 'The Triple Beehive' wouldn't fit through the doorway of Sweet Sensations.

Enough
was
enough.

So that's when Dad took Amy for her favourite Daddy Hairdo of all.

(And Amy **still** had more hair than Dad!)

Bunting

Children make bunting to decorate the workshop bench area, especially the fix-it bench. Draw their attention to the differences and similarities between the shapes and discuss where would be the best place to make holes. Children sort the cut-out material shapes into sets of the same shape. They choose a material shape and make two holes at the edge of the shape, using a hole punch. Children then thread the ribbon in and out of the holes to connect their shape to the rest of the line.

You need

- A collection of three different shapes (such as triangle, square and rectangle) cut from cotton material and mixed together
- Hole punches
- Long length of narrow gift wrapping ribbon threaded with blunt-ended plastic threading needle

Things to ask

How can we find out how many triangle shapes there are in the bunting?

Which material shapes will you choose to thread on the bunting?

How did you decide that shape was a rectangle?

Look, listen, note

Which children can

- identify and count a particular shape in the bunting?
- talk about the shapes they chose?
- sort the shapes into three sets?

Challenge

Children cut their own shapes from paper to make indoor bunting.

Children use shiny paper and make festival decorations.

Words to use

one, two, three … ten, triangle, square, rectangle, sort, set, group, edge

Maths learning

Number, shape and space

Counting to 10 everyday objects

Using the language of shape

Sorting objects into sets

Nail number line

Children make a reference number line for the workbench. They hammer some nails into thick pieces of balsa wood. Discuss which numerals the children want to make and supply a separate piece of wood and nails to each child. After they have hammered the nails into their wood, they count how many nails there are and write that number on the wood with a felt-tip pen. Together, assemble the pieces of wood in number order and display on a fence or wall. While engaged in this activity, children need to be carefully supervised by an adult and shown safe behaviour. Before displaying the nail number line, make sure that no nails have come through to the back of the balsa wood.

You need

- Children's hammers
- Nails
- Thick balsa wood
- Safety goggles
- Felt-tip pens

Things to ask

How can you find out the total number of nails you have hammered in?

What number will you write on your wood?

Where in the number line will you put your piece of wood?

Look, listen, note

Which children can

- count their nails to find out the total?
- recognise numerals to 10?
- successfully put their number nails in the correct place?

Challenge

Extend the number line to 10.

Thread a beadstring with the number of beads that matches the nail number and attach to the wood.

Words to use

one, two, three … five, number, numeral, how many?, count, altogether, total

Maths learning

Number, calculating

Saying and using number names

Recognising and writing numerals

Using the vocabulary of addition